Tale of the First Land

Daniel Reed

Table of Contents

Dedication

I'd like to dedicate this book to my mum, (Clare Reed) for standing by me, and believing in me, and supporting me no matter what I aim to accomplish.

Acknowledgement

I'd like to thank all the teachers and tutors that I have had in English, I would never have been able to write a story like this, without their support in learning to write and construct a sentence, I found my love of writing through them.

Chapter One: The Beginning

The beginning. Once, in a land, time had long forgotten, there was a great war when all creatures were at war. This war began when those from the kingdom of old began to dispute their roles in creating this world. Zaratheen, youngest of the three great gods and a beauty to behold, with her long dark hair which went down to her ankles and, flawless brown skin with absolutely no imperfections, she wore a long, white, silk gown which flowed as she walked, she was the pinnacle of beauty itself, she could not allow the fate her love, Venomos, a vile mistake of a creature, created by the forbidden love of two former gods, he was the polar opposite of Zaratheen, with his pale rotting green flesh, deathly stench, and bitter nature, Zaratheen's siblings, couldn't understand what she saw in him. He was to be exiled for creating orcs, ogres, and goblins. Orcs were violent, vile, hideous creatures with black skin, blood-red eyes, and filthy yellow teeth. They were unkillable to all but the gods. Ogres weren't much better, being large obese grey-skinned creatures that stood around ten feet tall, these creatures would devour anything that got on the wrong side of them. Finally, goblins were just as vile. These creatures were small, scrawny, almost skin and bone like things. They were completely hairless and had green skin, black teeth and nails, and yellow eyes. These creatures took pleasure in causing pain and suffering. They were carnivorous and would even eat their own if the food was scarce. But, the one who was to exile Venomos was Zaratheen's brother Zurothon.

Zurothon was a soldier, always wearing his solid gold armour, with his hair tied tightly in a bun. He could always be seen holding his sword as if he was ready to strike. Zurothon being the middle child of three, left to rule by Zowgore, father of time and space, Zurothon always felt he had something to prove, although his siblings never thought he should. Zaratheen consumed by her anger toward her brother, attempted to divert the situation and reported to her sister Zerthena; oldest of the three, Zerthena was wise but could be prone to rash decisions, she was also beautiful beyond words although, she felt no man would ever love her for, she had scars all over her body, Zurothon wasn't nice as a child, Zaratheen told Zerthena of a greater evil at work. Horrothors, The God of Death, was creating an army of darkness. Horrothors was an outcast of the gods, not being from the same family of gods but adopted by Zowgore from a fallen family. He always distanced himself from the others. His red skin and massive curled horns made him stand out from the others, so he made it that the other gods never really connected with him, even though Zerthena, Zurothon, and Zaratheen even Venomos would treat him like family. Zerthena confronted Horrothors hoping it wasn't true, but he admitted to the creation of his dark army, although it was far worse than she could've ever imagined.

Horrothors didn't just create an army. He created three plagues. The first was a plague of the blood which turned those it affected into creatures of the night, who feed on the blood of man, thus turning them into that which hunts them, the second was a plague of an open wound which cursed those it affected. On to be controlled by the moon to hunt man and spread the plague and the third, the third was a plague to end all, this plague affected the bodies of fallen man thus, rising them up from the dead to feed on the living and turn them to spread the plague. Zerthena asked Horrothors why he would create such a thing. Horrothors told her that man was a joke. The idea the creation is nothing more than that. This joke has grown old, he stated: "when man is created thou shalt release these plagues, and man shalt be eradicated before thou can even begin". Devastated by what she had heard, Zerthena could not allow these actions to go unpunished, she took immediate action and banished Horrothors from the kingdom of old, Horrothors didn't take likely to this and formed an alliance with Venomos, who also was exiled opposed to Zaratheen's attempt to stop her brother.

Upon leaving the kingdom of old Horrothors cried out with ferocity and anger, "thou shalt resent the day thou crossed Horrothors". The two exiled gods, feeling that they have the right to create the land, in the image they desire as much as the three great gods, waged war on the three to take the kingdom of old for themselves. Zaratheen stricken with grief from the betrayal of her love, who she had tried to save from being exiled after Venomos vowed to end Zaratheen and her siblings, Zaratheen called upon Morgisha, Morgisha was the elemental goddess, her entire body was like living smoke, her clothing was like water; shaped to look like long flowing gowns and, sparks of fire flew as she walked, Zaratheen asked Morgisha to create beings capable of fighting the army's the two dark gods had created. At which point Zerthena had created beings of her own. She raised trolls from the mountain and turned the tallest trees into giants to battle the dark army. However, it wasn't long before Zerthena lost control of her army, and they allied themselves with Horrothors and Venomos's forces. Zaratheen, who was tasked with the creation of man long before the fall of the kingdom of old, bestowed man with battle knowledge to fight the dark forces. Zurothon created dwarfs by moulding clay to the form of the perfect soldier to build weapons for man to battle the dark forces, and Morgisha created beings of magic to protect man. She did this by first taking the blood of man and mixing it with her own to create elves. Secondly, she took the blood of the elves and combined it with the blood of man to create the witches and wizards. She then took the blood of all to create pixies and fairies. Finally, she

4

took the blood of the pixies and the fairies and mixed it with the natural lad to create imps and sprites. The gods then sent all armies to Earth to battle each other. The winning army would determine which gods would rule the kingdom of old and create the world in the way they see fit. After the gods created the two forces, the forces of good and the forces of darkness, they no longer had any interaction with either side, well, all apart from one.

Twenty centuries these armies waged war against one other until man could take no more. Because of this, the high king of man called a truce with the uncrowned Prince of the Vampires, the dwarfs, and the magical beings, to find a peaceful resolution. After long and tiresome negotiations, they came to a resolve, they decided to split the land known as Arcadia into eight kingdoms, man would get the flat centre of the land to build their great cities, the magical beings would surround the land of man, with the mass of their land being to the north in the silver grass hills, dwarfs would surround the magic kingdom their land would mainly be to the south in the ever-growing woodlands, giants, and trolls were secluded east in the forests of Eeldoor, named after Eeldoor the Great, the first High King of man who fell fighting the forces of darkness in that very forest, they were cursed to be blind and deaf and their minds to be made simple for their traitorous betrayal. Goblins, ogres, and orcs were to be banished far south to the valley of the damned.

Once all the goblins, ogres, and orcs were in the valley, the witches and wizards charred the land, so it became a desert. They then announced that the land is known as the dead deserts of despair, so all who wander realise they have strayed too far. The vampires, due to their affliction to sunlight, requested the caved mountains as their dwelling, the king being grateful for the cooperation of the vampire prince, hastily agreed under the condition vampires only feed on small creatures and never again feed on man. Thus the vampires left for the caved mountains taking all manner of unholy beings with them. They travelled far north to the end of the land where they were to make their new beginning. The king then told the witches and wizards to cast a spell of eternal night over their land, so all know never to enter immediately. They released a spell that shrouded the land in eternal night, from the endless sea beyond the caved mountains back over the dark forest all the way to the edge of the magic kingdom. Neamwoy, the only God to bother with any of the beings the other gods had created, took pity on the forces of good and pulled creatures with magical properties from the land in the west, between the crystal sea and the border of the kingdom of dwarfs, this land became known as the arcane meadows. She then announced to all beings that only those with a good heart and intentions shall know of their existence; thus, only the good can see them. These creatures, large and small; strong or weak; kind or aggressive, were gifts nonetheless, so Neamwoy swore, any being who turned on them and meant them wrong would suffer a fate worse than death. Forty centuries passed with this arrangement holding strong never has and never would they be a more utopian land as the first land, the land of the eight kingdoms, but it couldn't last. Forty centuries later, the land of man had been split between four royal families. The first family were descendants of the first high king consisting of High King Laurence, High Queen Clare, and their children David, Daniel, Bethany, Rebecca, and Adam. High King Laurence ruled over the great city of Broadhall, he was a kind and caring king his people loved him and so did his family, there wasn't anyone in his city that didn't, High Queen Clare was kind but firm she never backed down from anyone, especially a man, many would joke that she ruled Broadhall not High King Laurence often overruling his decisions.

The second was Prince David's family. He was the first to be given land by his father and made king of the city of Alafurce. With his two sons, Aiden and Alex David was a just king. He would never pass judgement without knowing all the facts and often avoided conflict. However, he had a very quick temper where his kids were concerned, more specifically their safety, having so much responsibility as king he often never knew what they were doing or where they were, after losing his wife and mother to his boys, King

David centred himself on his duties as king rather than his duties as a father. The third family was queen Bethany's. She ruled the city of Eeldon with an iron fist, along with her three children, Niome, Noah, and Jacob. Queen Bethany's family was one to fear. Her children often manipulated the people into giving more in taxes. Noah would even attack those that couldn't pay although, with Bethany's to-be husband, things seemed to be taking a turn for the better. Finally, the fourth family was Prince Adam's who became King of Valewood, by winning the crown from his brother Daniel, Adam challenged Daniel to a battle of strength which was ultimately hand-to-hand combat. He did this because he felt Daniel didn't have what it took to rule a kingdom. When Adam took the Crown of Valewood, he took himself a wife and had four children, Jayden, Aria, Adam, and Elijah, but the citizens of Valewood didn't view Adam as their king. They felt that King Adam took the crown unfairly as he had military training where his brother did not, although his children were loved by all for their kindness and caring nature. Prince Daniel never really got to be a king, and losing to his brother was quite a hit on his pride. After the loss, Daniel went into exile somewhere in the ever-growing woodlands, although nobody knew where.

Chapter Two: The Fall of Magic

One evening in late summer, Prince Aiden and Prince Jayden were exploring near the border of the magic kingdom by the dark forest. Aiden and Jayden liked to explore and wanted to discover new lands when they were older. Aiden's wish could soon come true, being fifteen, nearly sixteen. He would soon be able to leave and explore new lands, although Jayden would have to wait for another three cycles before he could leave. They liked to pretend the places they went were never before seen lands, they were the first to discover them and would be famous in their fantasies, on this unfortunate day they climbed the wall pretending that it was a mountain, on the other side was this new land no one had ever seen when they were spotted by two guards from the Tower of Magic, they were taken captive and taken to Elven Queen Alecra. The Elven Queen's throne room resided in the Tower of Magic. Upon entering the throne room, the Prince's jaws dropped at the sheer beauty of it, the walls had a look of icy, diamond-like marble with a throne made from the same material, lined with silver and gold trimmings, the throne sat in the centre of the far wall, and there was a heavenly mural on the floor in front of it, there were large white pillars that stood around one hundred feet tall which circled the room, and they were lilac-coloured drapes of silk that swung from pillar to pillar; there were three stain glass windows around the room, the one on the left had an image of the great war, the one to the right depicted the alliance that was struck when the land was divided, the last one who was behind the throne was a map of all eight kingdoms. Suddenly a harrowing voice consumed the room "how dare you" the voice said, the Princes heads whipped forward to face the Elven Queen, the boys couldn't believe what they were seeing, the Elven Queen was such a beauty the two had never seen with her long black hair that almost touched her ankles, her fair white skin, her sparkling dark blue eyes that almost resembled sapphires and her blood-red lips, along with her snow-white robes that trailed behind her she really didn't look like the tyrant everyone thought she was, "how dare you threaten the safety of our kingdoms, with your attempt to breach the walls to the dark forest" said Alecra as she walked past the boys with such anger in her voice the two had never heard, Aiden stammered out "w..w..we" "silence" bellowed the Queen echoing through the room, taking her seat on her throne Alecra continued "I'm not interested in your pitiful excuses, if it wasn't for the alliance with your grandfather I would have you both in chains, as it is you both..." Alecra was abruptly interrupted by a sudden, loud, explosive sound that came from outside the tower. A guard rushed through the doors announcing to the queen that they were under attack. Alecra told the guard to take the Princes to the cells; she would deal with them later. As the guard took the two princes, Jayden shouted, "you have it all wrong. We're innocent. We didn't do anything," but the Queen just ignored them. Meanwhile, back in Alafurce, Prince Alex informed his father that his brother and cousin hadn't come home, his father brushed it off, not really paying attention, and told the young prince not to be concerned over it. His brother would be sixteen years of age. In two moons, he was more or less a man. Even though his father wasn't worried, the young prince still felt that something wasn't right. He made plans to find out what was going on and where his brother and cousin were. Later that evening, Alex snuck out of the castle to search for his brother and cousin. He used the secret passage that himself, Aiden, and Jayden had dug to the kingdom of beasts. That way, he could leave his father's kingdom undetected. After walking several miles through the dark passage, Alex finally arrived at the Kingdom of Beasts. He was immediately greeted by his good friend, a Griffin known as Thermasol. Alex told Thermasol that he was looking for his brother and cousin, the Griffin told Alex that they were last seen in the magic kingdom, Alex asked how he knew they'd be there the Griffin told Alex that the light spirits had told him, the light spirits were the souls of beasts that had long past only the pure of heart could see them. Thermasol told Alex that the light spirits had informed him about the attack on the magic kingdom, and Aiden and Jayden were in the Elven Queens dungeon. Alex insisted that they should do something to help. Thermasol told Alex to climb on his back; that was it for him. As an easily excited fourteen-year-old always looking for adventure, Alex jumped on Thermasols back without even a second thought. As Thermasol took flight, the young prince asked, "how are we going to get in the dungeons without being spotted" Thermasol told him that he was gifted with the ability to turn invisible. They would slip in completely unnoticed and rescue his brother and cousin. Alex asked curiously, "how will that help me?" Thermasol told the young prince that, as long as he was in contact with Thermasol, his abilities would also affect him. While they were on route to the magic kingdom to break the silence, Alex asked Thermasol what his name meant, confused Thermasol asked why he wanted to know; Alex said, "well, humans name their children after kings, queens, and figures of history, the people of the magic kingdom name their children after spirits and gods and, the dwarfs name their children after warriors or soldiers of valour so, what does your name mean?" Thermasol said "okay, well in my language my name means burning glory but, in your language, it means the soul of fire", "that's pretty cool," said Alex then followed with another question, "who named you", Thermasol said trying to keep to simple "well it might be difficult to understand, but you did, you see; I am your spirit guardian, when you were born I came to be", Alex was confused, he didn't understand how his birth was the cause of Thermasols existence, "just relax and enjoy the ride, we will be there soon" said Thermasol, so Alex did. As the two flew into the magic kingdom, they could see smoke billowing out of The Tower of Magic. Alex's heart skipped as he could only think of the worst things that could've happened to his brother and cousin. As they flew over the kingdom, Alex watched the crumbled and burning buildings pass below them, and he could feel the fear build in his stomach "get to the dungeons now!" Alex ordered. When the two arrived at the holding cells, Alex noticed that the cells were empty, he then spotted a guard who was barely alive. He approached the guard with a dagger in hand and asked the guard where his brother and cousin were. The guard struggling to breathe told Alex that they were taken by orcs. With a terrified look, Alex stuttered, "t.t.t.that's impossible, they're not real, they're made up to scare naughty children" the guard, barely holding on to his life, told the young prince that he couldn't be more wrong, choking on his last few breaths the guard told him to go to the Dwarf king Balomoor; he would help to rescue the missing princes and fight off the orcs, with that the guard died, Alex unsure how to process what was happening; turned to Thermasol and told him, if they were to fight they would need the help of his aunt in the city of Eeldon. Alex and Thermasol left the dungeon and took flight for the city of Eeldon. Alex asked Thermasol if the guard was telling the truth "do orcs really exist?" he asked, "I'm sorry but, yes, young prince, yes they do", said Thermasol. Alex couldn't believe it. He always thought they were myths. For the rest of the flight, Alex remained silent. He didn't know what to say. As the young prince and Thermasol approached the city of Eeldon, they heard the bells from the citadel of the crown ringing. The citadel of the crown was the name of the tower where the queen held trials for those she thought had committed a crime; they landed outside of his aunt's palace doors. He was met by his cousin Niome. Niome was horrid. She treats everyone like dirt beneath her feet. Being the oldest of her siblings, she was the next in line for the throne of Eeldon. Although she was only fourteen, she had to wait for another two cycles before she could take the throne. She asked Alex, with her usual arrogant attitude, what his business was. Alex told her that he needed to speak with his aunt urgently. Princess Niome told the young prince with an impertinent attitude; the queen was unavailable. Anything he needed from the queen she would be dealing with, Alex said aggressively, "I didn't care what she is busy with, I need to speak to her immediately; it is a matter of life and death", the princess completely unfazed repeated her previous statement. Alex was getting frustrated with his cousin. He turned to Thermasol, who gave a slight nod, then turned back to his cousin; grinned and, with a cocky attitude, said, "she's at the citadel of the crown, isn't she? I'll handle this myself", he then climbed back on

Thermasol and took off for the citadel of the crown on the other side of the city. Alex told Thermasol that he's alway hated her, Thermasol said "whether you like her or not she is still your family so, hate is a very strong word to use and nevertheless she was simply doing her job, you should think before condemning someone especially family", Alex thought about what he said for a moment then replied "I suppose your right", as the two arrived at the citadel of the crown Alex told Thermasol to go back to the arcane meadows, he burst through the doors and observed the queen about to execute a guard from the kingdom of magic, he shouted for her to stop, her guards, her council, the queen and the guard from the kingdom of magic all looked to Alex as he walked toward the queen, Alex asked what was going on, the queen arrogantly responded "it's none of your business but if you must know, this intruder was caught breaking into the palace", Alex said "but" but the queen cut him of and continued to say, "he was spouting a bunch of nonsense about orcs and an attack on the magic kingdom, if this were true, we would have known, and the alarm was not raised". Alex told the queen that it was all true, the kingdom of magic had fallen, and there was no one left alive in the kingdom. As the young prince said this, a guard walked in; approached the queen and handed her a letter, the queen took the letter, and after reading it, the queen looking horrified, said, "it appears that this guard was telling the truth, we must gather the Council of Crowns" she then told one of her guards to free the prisoner. She and Alex left to gather the Council of Crowns. Queen Bethany and Prince Alex summoned the Council of Crowns at the Court of Crowns in the city of Broadhall. They sent word for the Dwarf King, Balomoor; they allowed one day for him to arrive. Unfortunately, Queen Alecra had fallen in the attack. This left the court down by one crown, which meant any people of the magic kingdom who could have survived the attack now had no voice. All but King Balomoor appeared at the court of crowns, King Balomoor had sent a letter refusing the summoning. Queen Bethany stud in the centre of the Court of Crowns, which was a reasonably small circular room with seven thrones situated around the room, one for each ruler of the kingdom of man, one for the ruler of the dwarfs and one for the ruler of the magic kingdom, there was a desk that circled the room in front of the thrones made from black oak from the dark forest, and in the centre of the room was circular; slightly raised platform. Queen Bethany told the court of the attack on the magic kingdom, High King Laurence asked Queen Bethany "could you present any evidence of your claim that an attack took place as, the court has not heard any word from the magic kingdom of such a claim", she told the high king that not only did she have evidence but one of their own had seen the devastation, the High King intrigued, looked to each one of the council

16

members expecting one of them to voice their evidence, at which point Bethany called out for the young prince, prince Alex walked out to the centre of the court, King David looked at his father with a look of shock then angrily launched out of his seat and slammed his hands on the desk, he demanded the young prince to tell him what he was playing at, Alex equally aggressively told his father to let him speak, he then told the council of the attack on the magic kingdom and that it was orcs that committed the attack, the High King asked if Alex saw the orcs attack to which Alex regretfully said no, the High King then asked how he knew it was orcs the young prince told the High King that a guard in the magic kingdom told him, then as the High King thought about the young princes answer he asked, why the young prince was in the magic kingdom in the first place, Alex told him that his brother and cousin, Aiden and Jayden, had gone missing and his father didn't seem interested so he went looking for them himself, when his friend, Thermasol the griffin, told him that they were in the magic kingdom; in the elven queens dungeon, he went to rescue them but he wasn't expecting to find that it was orcs that were attacking, the young prince continued to say he always thought they were just myths. The High King looked at his son with a look of disgust. He asked why he never thought to inquire where his son and nephew were before he could answer. The High

King said: "never mind, I will deal with you soon as this matter is resolved".

The high king asked the court what they were going to do, at that moment Princess Rebecca stepped forward from behind her father and told the court that she would take her nephew to King Balomoor; they would get the weapons they needed to fight these orcs, King David aggressively shouted "NO" he then continued to say "I have already had one son taken by these horrid creatures, I'm not about to let another get taken" with that comment King Adam responded telling King David to take his seat, he then addressed King David directly and said "you seem to forget that my son was taken too, if your youngest knows something that will help return our boys, it is his responsibility to assist" Rebecca raised her voice making it known that, if the young prince was the only one who had seen first hand what the orcs were capable of, only he could convince King Balomoor to help, as King David attempted to argue with his sister he could only get out "I won't allow" before the High King stated with his voice soaring over everyone else's "so shall it be, Rebecca you shall take Alex to King Balomoor and the rest of this court will fortify the kingdom, no possible attacks will devastate this kingdom the way the magic kingdom has been devastated", King David simply said "but, Father…" to which the High King cut him of before he could speak and told him that the decision was final. As Rebecca and Alex left the court, she told him to prepare to leave, and they wouldn't be returning until they had rescued his brother and cousin. Alex, looking confused, said, "I thought we were going to the dwarf kingdom" Rebecca pulled Alex to one side and told him that they were going to the dwarf kingdom, but she wasn't going to just stand by and watch some want-to-be-hero, attempt to rescue her nephews and fail miserably, she told him that wasn't the general of her father's army for nothing, and he would soon see why on that Rebecca walked of leaving Alex wondering what she meant by that last comment or worse what she had planned. Alex and Rebecca left on horseback at first light to head for the dwarf kingdom. Alex didn't say anything to his aunt, but he was sure she was going to start a full out war. After all, she was known as the general of death among her soldiers. After a silent hour's ride, they arrived at the edge of what remained of the magic kingdom. They both just stood still for a moment and looked at the sheer deviation. Alex asked his aunt why they were there. Looking confused, he asked, "weren't we meant to be going to the dwarf kingdom," Rebecca told the young prince that she just had to see it for herself. Alex then asked how they were going to stop an army that could devastate such a powerful kingdom in less than one night. Rebecca told the young prince with arrogance in her voice that this army may be powerful, but they have never messed with the likes of her. She continued to tell him, "I will devastate their entire existence in half the time they devastated the magic kingdom" after that, they carried on with their journey to the dwarf kingdom. The two arrived at the gates to the dwarf kingdom after a days ride. Although they were exhausted, their troubles had only begun. As the two approached the large wooden gates, a dwarf opened a small panel in the gate. He demanded they holt and identify who they were and what their business was. Rebecca responded, saying, "I am princess Rebecca, heir to the throne of Broadhall and general of my father's army, I demand to speak with your king immediately" the dwarf scoffed at Rebecca and slammed the pannal shut, Rebecca dismounted her horse and began banging repeatedly on the gates, the dwarf opened the pannal and told her "you may as well leave, dwarfs didn't deal with your kind", Rebecca drew her sword and said to the dwarf intending to intimidate him "you will open this gate and we will speak with your king you impertinent half man", the dwarf laughed hysterically and closed the pannal, Alex asked his aunt what they were going to do if they couldn't get through the gates, before Rebecca could answer the gates opened, the same dwarf walked out with a large battle axe in his hands and said with an arrogant and aggressive tone "if you want to get through these gates you're going to have to get through me", the dwarf then began to swing his heavy axe with incredible speed and force, Rebecca ducked and dodged the dwarfs swings while Alex could only watch in fear for his aunt, after multiple attempts to land a blow on the experienced general, Rebecca managed to get behind the dwarf and held her sword to his throat, the dwarf dropped his axe and told her that she had earned the right to enter the kingdom, he was merely testing her to see if she could prove her warriors spirit, Rebecca; in a battle rage didn't lower her weapon, gripping the dwarf tighter and pulling her sword closer to his throat; ready to slaughter the dwarf, she screamed "you will burn in the pits of the demonic realm" but, before she could slit the dwarfs throat, Alex let out a blood curdling scream of fear shouting "NO" to stop his aunt from killing the dwarf, hearing her nephews cry of fear she pulled out of her rage and lowered her weapon, the dwarf shaken by the sheer fury but hiding it well, told them that the king didn't take nicely to humans in his kingdom but, as she was willing to take a life just to gain an audience it shows that their business was not one that was merely a cordial visit, Rebecca mounted her horse and the two made their way to the dwarf kings castle. Alex asked his aunt, "what happened back there" but Rebecca just remained silent. He then asked if she thought the dwarf was really testing her, to which she responded, "that pathetic half-man was simply a coward and couldn't accept defeat" the two continued up the path toward the dwarf king's castle, Alex was beginning to see why his aunt had been kept from battle by her father, her rage was too aggressive even for war. Upon entering the

21

dwarf king's castle, which looked older than time itself, with crumbled walls, Ceilings and columns; overgrown shrubbery of trees, bushes, weeds and vines, it had a cool, dank feel as they passed through it, suddenly the two heard an echoing deep voice cascade through the halls that demand they leave, the voice continued to echo "your kind aren't welcome in my kingdom, leave while I allow it" said the voice, Rebecca laughed softly then replied, "I have already bested your guard at the gates, don't make me do it again" she continued to say, "I am princess Rebecca, heir to the throne of Broadhall and general of my father's army, we require assistance on a very important matter" the voice remained silent for a moment; Rebecca broke the silence simply saying impatiently "well", the dwarf king walked out from behind a column, he was a withered old dwarf with long silver hair and wrinkles so deep they were like crevices in the skin, he used an axe as a walking stick and wore the pelt of a black bear, like a cloak over his armour which was so rusted it didn't seem to even be able to protect him. As he slowly hobbled toward Rebecca and Alex, the dwarf king said to Rebecca, "I know who you are, and I know of the matter which you speak. As I told your father in a letter responding to the court summoning, I don't have the slightest interest in the matters of man" Rebecca responded with teeth grit, saying, "so you're the dwarf king, please assist us in this matter", Balomoor turned his back to

Rebecca and said "begone we're done here", Alex looked at his aunt and could see the anger build on her face, suddenly Rebecca lunged at king Balomoor sword drawn and demanded his assistance, Balomoor turned to find Rebecca's sword within inches of his face, with a sudden burst of incredible speed and power, that both Rebecca and Alex had never seen nor expected form one of such old age, King Balomoor swiped Rebecca's sword away then began to barrage Rebecca with endless swings of his axe while telling her, "your arrogance will be your end". While Rebecca repeatedly blocked him and tried to find her moment to strike back, Alex could only stand and watch as it became evident that Balomoor was going to win and ultimately end his aunt's life. He began to feel something build inside him. He thought to himself. It wasn't fear. It felt like anger, but it was something different. Small sparks of energy began to arc across Alex's fingers. Then, with a ferocious burst, Alex shouted for them to stop and raised his hands toward them. He emitted an explosive blast of energy. He separated Rebecca and Balomoor, throwing them in opposite directions. Alex looked at his hands in pure shock, not able to conceive what had just happened. Rebecca looked at Alex, also shocked by what had happened and asked Alex how he could have magic, saying it wasn't possible for him to have magic. King Balomoor laughed intensely while he brought himself to his feet and said, "oh, how naive you must be" confused, Rebecca arrogantly asked what he was talking about, Balomoor highly amused with a sarcastic tone, she asked Rebecca "do you mean to tell me that you didn't know that his mother, was-a-dark-witch!" Rebecca remained silent she didn't know what to say, Balomoor told Alex and Rebecca to follow him, Rebecca lifted herself off the floor, and the two followed Balomoor. He led them to the armoury. It was covered from floor to ceiling with all kinds of weapons, shields and armour. Balomoor walked over to a cabinet and took out a sword and shield. He then handed them to Alex. He told the young prince that they were made for the first high king, they were crafted in the great war, but they were never used. He told him that they were the lightest and strongest ever made; they were meant to be enchanted to slay orcs but never were. Alex asked, "how could we enchant them since the magic kingdom no longer stands?", Balomoor told him that there was one of two ways, either find the four elemental dragons. However, they haven't been seen since the separation of the kingdoms or find the grand high witch Susan. Alex looked at Balomoor with confusion and said sarcastically, "what part of there's-no-body-left don't-you-get?" Balomoor shook his head in disgrace and said to Rebecca, "this boy's arrogance could rival even yours", although feeling relentless to tell the prince, after he arrogantly interrupted him, Balomoor thought to himself (they will only pester me until I tell them what I know), he then told Alex that the grand high witch left the magic kingdom somewhat four decades back. The last he heard, she was living somewhere in the forest of Eeldoor, but finding her wouldn't be their hardest task. Avoiding the giants and trolls would be their most challenging burden. Alex thanked the dwarf king then Alex and Rebecca took their leave, but just as they went to exit the armoury, Balomoor told Alex to be mindful of his newfound abilities. Magic is not something to be toyed with. They were consequences for using such power as a plaything. The two then left the dwarf kingdom for their journey to the forest of Eeldoor.

It went without saying out loud but, each turn led them further and further away from their goal, which was solely to rescue Aiden and Jayden but, it seemed less and less likely, especially to Rebecca, being older and being a soldier she knew they were running out of time.

Chapter Three: Worsening Times

While Alex and Rebecca were on their journey to find the grand high witch, Aiden and Jayden were in the orc kingdom trying to find a way to escape. As the two were sitting in a cage suspended off the ground, Aiden told Jayden that he had a plan to get out, but it wasn't going to be easy. Jayden told him it was pointless. They were done for. Aiden encouraged him to stay strong; they were going to get out; this wasn't going to be the end of them. Just then, an orc shook the cage and hit it with his sword. The orc told them with a screeching voice that was enough to drive any man insane; be quiet. Aiden whispered, "I'm going to try and grab the keys of that disgusting creature, but I need you to distract him" Jayden, worried that his cousin's plan would just make things worse, hesitantly agreed, nodding his head, "good," said Aiden continuing to say "when he comes back; distract him, I'll get the keys". As the orc walked back toward them, Jayden told him to give them something to eat. They were hungry.

The orc griped Jayden through the cage and said to him, "starve, I'm dying for a good meal" while the orc was occupied, Aiden slipped his hand through the bottom of the cage, he gently grabbed the keys, then stuffed them up his shirt, the orc threw Jayden against the back of the cage, the orc walked away laughing maniacally, unbeknownst to him

Aiden had taken his keys. Later that evening, Aiden unlocked the cage, the two of them began slowly making their way through the sleeping orcs. Just as they thought they had escaped, Aiden, not paying attention, walked into the back of an ogre. Startled, the ogre thought it was an orc, growling he said "watch where you are walking stupid orc", but as the ogre turned around he saw it wasn't an orc, the ogre sounded the alarm waking the orcs, the orcs grabbed the princes then clamped their hands in chains; suspending them off the floor "try getting out of this" screeched the same orc that seemed to like terrorising the young princes. Aiden looked to Jayden and apologised. He told him; they should have just stayed in the cage. He was right to think his plan would fail, he was sorry, but now he may have only made things worse.

Meanwhile, Alex and Rebecca made haste and had reached the edge of the forest of Eeldoor. On their way, neither one mentioned Alex's newfound abilities. As they entered the forest of Eeldoor, they could hear loud crashing and banging in the distance, Rebecca told Alex that the forest was riddled with giants and trolls, and if he weren't careful, he wouldn't know they were there until they were on top of him, the young prince confused asked how he wouldn't know if they were so big, Rebecca told him that the forest was so thick it was almost impossible to see anything, also the giants and trolls blended into the forest, Alex asked if there was any else he should know about the forest, Rebecca told him that some people have spoken of gremlins in the forest but, she personally didn't believe in gremlins nonetheless; he should be mindful of his surroundings. While they slowly and carefully made their way through the forest, they saw giants and trolls pass by them, each time being as quiet as they could not startle either of them. The last thing they needed was to startle a giant who could stomp them into the ground or a troll who could squash them effortlessly. Alex noticed something moving through the trees and told Rebecca. She made a joke of it, saying, "I think it might be a gremlin", then Rebecca noticed the figure move through the trees, they dismounted and quietly moved closer, they spotted a man trying to hide behind a tree and Rebecca told him to holt, the man started to run, so the two began to chase him, he led them to a small wooden cottage nestled away in a thick patch of trees, Rebecca slowly entered the cottage and Alex nervously followed not sure what to expect. When they entered the cottage, it was dark and hard to move without walking into something suddenly, candles lit all around the cottage, and the door slammed shut behind them. The room was full of pots, veils, jars and all sorts of creepy looking things, from the floor to the ceiling and all over the walls. A woman's voice came for the back of the cottage saying "speak quickly or be gone" they looked to see a woman in a long black hooded robe, she walked toward them followed by a scrawny timmed looking girl, Alex asked if she was the grand high witch, the woman snapped sharply "who wants to know", Alex told her speaking very quickly "im Alex prince of Alafurce and, the woman is my aunt princess Rebecca of Broadhall, we need your help to enchant a sword and shield the dwarf king gave me, we need them to fight the orcs and rescue my brother and cousin", the woman lowered her hood to reveal a kind looking older woman, with long dark hair and a loving smile, her skin was olive colored; thought worn not exactly wrinkled, although her eyes were a very deep blue they felt like they were looking straight into your sole, she told them that she was the grand high witch Susan and the girl was her apprentice Samantha, Samantha was tall and scrawny, she had long light brown hair and skin as white as sheets she seend to cower behind Susan. Alex said, quite surprised, "you're not what I was expecting," Susan, curious about his statement, asked him what exactly he was! Expecting, with a smirk, Alex replied, "well… worts, wrinkles, maybe even green skin" Samantha chuckled slightly, covering her mouth with her hand, and Rebecca smacked Alex across the back of his head and told him to show some respect, Susan scowled at Alex and told him that he had some cheek. Rebecca spotted the man they followed. He was in the corner of the room, peering from behind a curtain. Rebecca asked Susan who he was and told her they followed him in after spotting him spying on them in the forest. Susan told her that it was just her son Alan and not to worry, he's just very wary of people as they don't get many visitors. Alan was quite old, somewhere in his late forties to early fifties, but he seemed to act somewhat like a child. Alex asked Susan if he was mongified or something. Rebecca gave Alex another slap and told him it was going to start hurting him before it started to hurt her. Susan told Alex that Alan wasn't like other people. He had problems that made him act different, but it didn't mean he wasn't like everyone else. He was still a person, and he should be treated the same as other people. Samantha added, saying, "for all you know, he could be a powerful warlock. You never truly know!" Rebecca asked Susan if she could enchant the sword and shield, Susan told her that she could, but she would need a plant that was difficult to get. Rebecca felt that she wasn't going to like the answer asked, "what plant do you need, and where could I get it", Susan said regretfully, "it's called the Dracula Vampira orchid, but it only grows in the dark forest" Rebecca losing her temper, slammed her fist on a table knocking everything off it and raised her voice, saying, "we don't have time for these shortsighted quests, every moment we waste only puts my nephews in further peril" Susan's voice deepened as the room dimmed. The wind began to hurl through the cottage, although the windows and doors were shut. She told Rebecca if she was to rescue her nephews, she would need to get the plant. Without it, she would die before she would get anywhere near the orcs' kingdom. Realising that she was outmatched, Rebecca backed down. She agreed to retrieve the plant and asked what it looked like. Susan told her that it was a black and yellow orchid, Rebecca and Alex went to leave, but as they were just about to go, Susan told Rebecca that she had to complete this task alone. It was far too dangerous for the young prince.

Alex told Rebecca to go. He would wait there. The sooner she got the plant, the sooner they could save Aiden and Jayden. After Rebecca left, Susan told Alex that she could sense they were hiding something. Alex pursed for a moment, then said quietly with a regretful tone, "I have magic" Susan told him not to be so regretful magic could be a blessing. She asked him curiously, "how long have you had magic" before he could answer, she added, "were you born with it or did you learn it," Alex told her that he only found out recently; he cast magic to stop his aunt and Balomoor from fighting. Susan then offered to teach Alex to use his magic. Alex hastily declined and told her that magic was outlawed in his kingdom. If he learnt to use magic, he would be exiled. Susan turned away and said, "to fear magic is to fear yourself. If you fear yourself, you can never truly wield this gift, a gift that has been given to you" Alex stepped forward, reaching out for Susan as she began to walk away and told her to wait. He then told her that he supposed it couldn't hurt to learn a few spells. Susan turned to face Alex and said, "if you truly wish to learn how to harness the art of magic, you must know that all magic comes with a price, a price that you may not always be willing to pay," the young prince told the witch with an arrogant attitude that he had more than enough money to cover any cost, the witch laughed and told the young prince that it wasn't that sort of price, she continued to tell him that the price of dark magic will destroy the body and blacken the heart. Curious to what she told him, the young prince asked what the price for that show with his aunt cost her, Susan paused for a moment then lifted her sleeve to reveal that her hand had turned black as if the flesh was dead, she told Alex that she had used dark magic to scare his aunt which meant, she would have to pay a dark price, Alex asked if magic would help save his brother and cousin, she told him that it may not help save them, but it would help get them close enough to save them, the young prince thought for a moment then then told her, he was willing to pay the price, whatever it may be, Susan then told the young prince that she would teach him a spell to focus his magic, Alex asked her why he needed a spell stating that he didn't use a spell in Balomoors castle, she told him that spells only focus the magic not create it, without them the magic is more spontaneous and random, the young prince asked what she was going to teach him, Susan told him that she was only going to teach him a spell to focus the cast he already knew, she wasn't teaching him a new cast. Alex asked why she wasn't going to teach him something new. Susan told him, "you need to learn to control the magic you already have before learning something new" Alex accepted her offer. However, he felt cheated as he thought she would teach him all sorts of magic, but the young prince understood why the witch wasn't going to teach him more than just control. Susan took the young prince outside and told him to focus on the direction he wanted to cast his magic. She told him calmly to ground himself and be one with the land, the air, and the life force in all things, to feel the water flow through the roots of the trees, to feel the beating heart of the birds in the trees, she told him to listen for the flutes of a butterflies wings and the echo of a gentle breeze, to see the far of land which the eye can't see and look beneath the waves of the raging sea. Alex looked at Susan, confused, and said with an attitude, "how am I meant to do that? It's impossible", Susan told him sternly to focus. She told him to close his eyes and clear his mind, Alex did what she said, and a moment later, he told her he could feel the water and beating hearts, he could hear butterflies' wings and the breeze echo through his ears, he could see the kingdom of beasts as if he was there and he could see fish swim beneath the waves. Susan told him to point in the direction he wanted to cast and clearly say, "savrus persorem victorium vecks", Alex did exactly what he was told, but nothing happened. Susan told him that he had to feel it, so he gave it another go.

His voice rumbled through the trees as he recited the words "savrus... Persorem... victorium... vecks", and in a concentrated burst of energy, Alex blasted a tree out of the ground. He was shocked at the sheer force behind a concentrated cast. Susan told him to keep practising, and he did right throughout the night, not resting for sleep, food, or water. He could only think of one thing if he perfected his magic, he could save his brother and cousin. While Alex was secretly practising his magic, Rebecca had made her way to the dark forest. It was easier to just go north of the forests of Eeldoor. The two forests meet in the north. As she entered the dark forest, she knew she was being watched. She could feel it. It was like she could feel the eyes of something press against her very soul. Her skin crawled with the fear of what it could be. As the warm wind blew across the back of her neck, it felt like a breath of something right behind her. It made her turn around; a sword was drawn, then turned again and again. She didn't like this feeling. All Rebecca wanted to do was leave. Sheafing her sword, she told herself, "get the plant and go, get the plant and go" she kept thinking it repeatedly in her head. As she got deeper into the dark forest, Rebecca saw hordes of walking dead. She decided to keep her distance and slowly, carefully, and quietly make her way further into the dark forest. As she did, she saw wolfmen just past the hordes of walking dead. Rebecca couldn't do it. She couldn't take anymore, she turned back to leave and saw the

34

plant she'd been looking for, quickly and quietly Rebecca pulled it out and stuffed it in a bag but, in her hast she'd scratched herself on a thorn, a single drop of blood dripped from her hand and hit the floor the wolfmen began to howl, Rebecca looked and saw they were coming toward her;

she began to run, running as fast as she could, not looking back but knowing that the wolfmen were gaining on her, almost within reach, one of the wolfmen lept toward her, suddenly another wolfman appeared, tackling the other one. Rebecca dove to the floor and looked to see. This wolfman was different. This one was black as night and had eyes as blue as the sky. Wolfmen are usually grey with black eyes. The black wolfman growled at Rebecca as if to tell her to leave. Not bothering to question it, she got to her feet and ran for her life. She wasn't stopping, not until she was back in the forests of Eeldoor.

Chapter Four: An Unlikely Friendship

While Rebecca was on her quest and Alex was learning to use magic, the two captured princes were beginning to lose hope of being rescued, tired, hungry, and trapped in the midst of hordes upon hordes of sleeping orcs, goblins, and ogres. Early hours of the morning, Jayden was trying to keep Aiden awake. He was beginning to pass out from the overwhelming hunger and thirst. Jayden feared Aiden wouldn't wake if he let him sleep. Although he was fighting the urge to sleep himself, Jayden told Aiden to hold on and reassured him that they would be rescued. Just then, a pale white orc approached, offering food and water. The orc told the two princes that he wasn't like the rest. He told them that he would try to help them as much as possible, but the rest of the orcs could never know, for all of their safety would be at risk. The sleeping orcs became restless as daylight drew near. The pale orc told the princes he'd return with more food and water at nightfall. As the day passed, Jayden and Aiden watched as the orcs abused and tormented the pale orc, they would call him names pointing out that he looked different to other orcs and, because he was smaller than the other orcs they would push him over and throw him around while laughing at him, the princes could see how the pale orc despised his own kind for the way they treated him, when night fell the pale orc returned true to his word, he brought food and water and told the princes that there was word amongst the ogres and goblins, that a young prince was going to attempt to rescue them, along with a general from the human army but, the ogres planed to stop this alleged rescue attempt, nevertheless getting excited Aiden said quite loudly "that's my brother and aunt, I knew they would come, I knew it" the pale orc told Aiden to be quiet or he'd wake the other orcs, Jayden asked the pale orc what his name was, the orc told them his name was Graw, he told them he was going to help them escape if he could, but there was one condition, they had to take him with them and allow him refuge in their kingdom, Jayden looked to Aiden in hope that he would decide whether they should take the orc with them but, rather than saying anything Aiden simply give a slight nod; Jayden told Graw that they could take him with them but it wasn't their choice to grant him refuge, it was up to the council of crowns, Graw's eyes sunk for he thought these humans would grant his wishes, Jayden continued to tell him that they would tell their fathers of his acts; hopefully that would be enough for them to make a decision in is favour, Graw agreed woefully and said "if that is all you can do then hopefully, it might just be enough" Graw left telling them he'd return in an hour but they must do everything he tells them if their to escape. After the hour had passed, the two began to wonder where Graw was and if he would return, the night passed, and the morning drew near. The two saw no sign of Graw. It was obvious he wasn't going to return.

After a day and two nights Rebecca returned with the plant, Alex had practiced the spell that Susan taught him and mastered it, although he kept quiet about it not letting on to Rebecca what he'd been up to, Rebecca handed the plant to Susan who dropped it into a large cauldron, one that she had already prepared with the rest of the ingredients for the charm, she told Rebecca to put the sword and shield in the cauldron, almost instantly the cauldron began to shake and glow then in a burst of light, the cauldron vanished leaving the sword and shield floating in mid air with a golden glow, Susan took the sword and shield and handed them to Alex and Rebecca, she told them the shield would protect them from any attack no matter how powerful and, it would even protect them from the harshest of weathers, she then told them the magic in the sword made it so nothing can damage it, it only takes in that which makes it stronger, furthermore the magic had made the sword so sharp that it could cut through anything, Rebecca thanked Susan and told Alex that they best make their way, stating they had no time to spear, she then left the cottage but, before Alex could follow Susan asked him to give her a moment, she reached into a small bag on a table and handed him a crystal, and a book, she told him that the crystal had the power to transport them away from danger but, it could only be used once and only ever once for, it would disintegrate after it had been used so to use it wisely, the book was her first spell book, it seemed only fit for it to be his first spell book, with that Alex thanked her and left the cottage. The two began to make their way to the dead deserts of despair. Rebecca asked Alex if he had asked Susan about his mother and whether Balomoor was telling the truth. Alex, unsure of what his aunt would think or say if he told her the truth said, "I know the law. I know if I indulge in magic, I would be exiled, so I just left it" Rebecca simply remained silent, but they both knew he was right. When Alex and Rebecca approached the dead deserts, Rebecca dismounted her horse. She began to set camp in a small woodland by the desert. Alex asked her what she was doing and told her that they needed to keep going. Rebecca, while continuing to set camp, said, "nightfall will soon be on us. If we enter the desert now, we will surely lose our way. We can make camp here and leave at first light", Alex unsympathetically agreed. However, he'd rather just hurry and get to his brother and cousin.

Later that evening, Aiden and Jayden were still captive in the orc horde, Graw didn't return, and the princes knew that he must have been caught. Usually, the orcs were quiet at night, but this night was different. They could hear rawing and howling, growling and screaming. It was all coming from just over the hill, and all the two could see were thick clouds of smoke and a red glow. Then suddenly, the shadow of a horned figure appeared in the smoke, and the two began to fear what would happen. All kinds of thoughts were going through their minds when the noise died down. The red glow dimmed, and the princes were approached by an orc with his goblin servant and two ogres, who the princes thought could have been his personal guards because they were the only ogres the two princes had seen that wore armour.

The orc grinned with a maniacal look on his grotesque face, then dropped a sack in front of them. He then walked away laughing equally as maniacal, Aiden demanded to know what was going on and what was in the sack, the orc turned his head back to side glance the princes and simply said "your hope", the orc then walked away while continuing his maniacal laugh, as the orc walked away with the ogres, the goblin grabbed the bottom of the sack and began to yank it until the content emptied, the two princes look to see their friend Graw ripped apart, their faces sunk as they realised why he never returned their worst fears had come true, he had indeed been caught attempting to help them escape but now, what was going to happen to them they thought, as the goblin ran of cackling he began to chant in a high pitch and irritating voice "princes, princes gonna die, tooth for tooth, eye for eye, kill you friends when they arrive, princes, princes then you die" as the horrid creature ran of he'd repeat it between cackles, the two princes where terrorfied what the

40

orcs and ogres had planned but, they knew they couldn't do anything to stop them.

As the morning drew near, Rebecca and Alex began to set down. As the sun rose over the horizon, they began to ride. They were eager to reach the orcs' kingdom before the next nightfall. This was their final stretch to save their family from the grasp of those vile creatures. As they made their way through the dead deserts of despair, Rebecca told Alex that there are stories that say the dead deserts of despair used to be a wonderful land and full of life, but after the great war, it became what it is today a baron waste full of death and decay, Alex couldn't believe that this dreary; desolate place was once a wonderful land, he asked Rebecca what happened to it, she told him "the stories don't say, but some believe that it was something to do with our ancestors", Alex asked her if she believed it, but Rebecca didn't say. Instead, she responded by saying that all she knows is the great war was a very dark time, and nobody truly knew what really happened during that time. To change the subject, Rebecca said to Alex, "we best make hast if we want to reach the orcs before nightfall. We can't waste another day", Alex agreed, and the two began to charge through the desert. Nothing was going to stop them. By midday, they had reached the end of the desert; Rebecca dismounted and perched on the edge of an incredibly wide and deep chasm. She waved Alex over and whispered to keep quiet and stay low. As they looked down into the chasm, Rebecca told Alex that this place was known as the valley of the damned. She told him it was where Aiden and Jayden were being held captive. Rebecca spotted a way in, it was to the east of the valley, but it was overrun with ogres. The problem was it seemed to be the only way in that wouldn't result in immediate death. Rebecca whispered to Alex, "we need to make a plan. Just charging in would result in imminent death" Alex thought for a moment, then said, "let's use their own tactics and attack while they sleep", Rebecca agreed and smiled, thinking to herself; he would make a great general one day with a mind like his, the two waited at the top of the valley until the time was right. They would make their strike but would only have one opportunity to do so. As light began to dim and night grew near, Rebecca and Alex watched the orcs and goblins march toward a clearing in the west of the valley, although the orcs and goblins couldn't be seen in the clearing fires could be seen burning over the top, suddenly in a massive burst of flames a large horned figure appeared, Rebecca and Alex's faces whitened and the life seemed to leave their eyes, as the figure emerged out of the flames to reveal the ancient god of death Horrothors, Horrothors stood larger than life in the center of the clearing, he let out an almighty raw as wormlings circled the sky above him, nobody truly knew what wormlings were although everyone knew they were a creature to fear; large, winged, levery skinned serpents that spat a venom that would slowly drive you insane before ultimately killing you, these creatures were an abomination to nature, that very moment Rebecca and Alex realised that things were far worse than they could have ever thought possible, Rebecca shouted at Alex to move saying "this is it, we strike now".

Chapter Five: The Death of a Prince

While Rebecca and Alex waited for their moment to strike, Aiden and Jayden watched the orcs and goblins march past them. A mere five orcs remained to keep watch over the two princes. Aiden demanded to know what was going on and why they were all leaving. One of the orcs backhanded Aiden across the face and told him to be quiet. He told Aiden that they would be rid of the princes before the night was through. Jayden had reached his limit with the orcs and began to aggressively shout, saying, "we have been abused, mistreated, and starved for almost a week, we are princes, royalty among men, and we will stand for this no more", the orc growled and grabbed the chains holding them up then threw them both to the floor, he told another orc to unlock their shackles. As soon as they were free, Jayden lunged at the orc that hit Aiden, the same one that had given them all the grief since the moment they arrived, but, before Jayden could even grab the orc, he plunged his sword into the prince's chest.

At that moment, Alex and Rebecca were fighting their way through the ogres. Just as they go through, Alex sees the orc kill Jayden. He let out a blood-curdling scream from the pit of his soul, screaming "NO", Alex raised he had to cast the spell Susan had taught him, speaking the words "savrus persorem victorium vecks", he sent four of the five orcs

44

flying. Aiden ran to Jayden and held him in his arms. With his final breath, Jayden muttered, "I'm sorry" Aiden sobbed while holding the body of his cousin as the orc laughed. The orc then placed his sword on the back of Aiden's neck and told him that he was next. While the tears streamed down Aiden's face, the cries turned to a devilish scream as Aiden grabbed the orc's wrist. Suddenly the life force drained from the orc; travelled through Aiden and into Jayden. The orc fell to the floor lifeless as Jayden gasped for his breath. They both got to their feet and ran toward Alex and Rebecca. Alex grabbed Jayden and asked what happened, telling him that he could swear he saw him die. Jayden, with shock and excitement, said, "it was Aiden; he used magic and brought me back". As Jayden told Alex that Aiden had saved him, Aiden called out Alex's name. Alex looked to see Aidan staring at his hands with a terrified look. Aiden looked at Alex, Jayden, and Rebecca, terrified, and said regrettably, "I'm so sorry I didn't mean to do it... forgive me... please", the three could only watch as his skin began to turn black, the colour in his eyes turned a greyish black, and his hair turned the same greyish colour, suddenly in a flash of black light Aiden disappeared, Jayden screamed out "NO, AIDEN" while reaching to where Aiden was stood but Alex pulled him back, he told him in a panicked voice it was too late, he was gone, there was nothing they could do, Jayden began crying "no... but... no" Alex shouted while pulling him away "he used dark magic and paid the price we need to go", Jayden turned away, and the three ran for the valley's exit. Rebecca got ahead of Alex and Jayden and grabbed the horses, she met Alex and Jayden at the top of the chasm, and they quickly rode away, not looking back or stopping for a rest, not until they reached the woodland on the other side of the dead deserts of despair did they stop when they finally stopped to rest the following morning, Alex immediately burst into tears and fell to his knees, Rebecca told him to stand up and be a soldier, but Alex just cried "my brothers gone", Rebecca told him that they can still save him but, it will be much harder and take much longer than they thought, although she did think to herself it was hopeless, she needed them to be strong, she couldn't carry the weight of all their sorrow back home, not when another great war was on the verge of breaking out.

When they arrived back in the kingdom of man the next day, Rebecca wasted no time gathering the council of crowns. She told her father of the dangers to come, the horrors they witnessed, and that the ancient God of Death Horrothors had risen before them. Suddenly the doors to the council chamber swung open, and the uncrowned prince of the vampires walked in. Everyone's heads whipped to face the vampire prince and followed as he walked toward the centre of the court to stand beside Rebecca. The uncrowned prince of the vampires was, without doubt, one of the most, if not the most terrifying thing any of them had ever seen. His skin was chalky white and slightly see-through, which made it possible to see his veins, his eyes were entirely black like cole with blood-red pupils, and he had faint red rings around his eyes. His fingernails were long and black like little black knives. He wore long black robes with red trim and a long black cape that trailed behind him as he walked. Rebecca demanded to know what he was doing there and told him that he wasn't welcome in the presence of royalty. The vampire prince just ignored her as if she wasn't even there. She then called him a vile blood-sucking parasite. It was pretty obvious Rebecca despised this man. The vampire prince, without looking at her, said very calmly, "I am royalty, you pestilent child. Now, hold your tongue, or..." he then turned his head to face Rebecca and continued saying very sharply, "I'd gladly hold it for you when I remove it from your mouth". The vampire prince addressed the high king directly and told him that he was there to help. Rebecca said with the utmost anger in her voice, "HELP! HELP! Where were you when the magic kingdom fell? Where were you when we were fighting ogres, goblins, and orcs? Or, what about when I had to sneak around the dark forest to find a stupid plant? I know! How about when my nephew turned into an evil warlock? Where was your help then"? She then turned away and waved her hand to dismiss him, saying, "Be gone, vampire, you're clearly not needed", the vampire prince hissed at Rebecca and while reaching toward her face with aggression in his voice, he said, "do not call me a vampire! Haemonemic is the term I prefer. Now I've told you once, child hold your tongue!" the high king shouted "enough!" which echoed through the court. The two looked at the high king and ceased their squabbling; the vampire prince bowed to the high king and said "forgive me, your highness", he said calmly to Rebecca, "do you think you left the dark forest without any help? Should I remind you how my friend helped you? He stopped the Wolfmen who hunted you and aided your escape. Do you seriously think that was a coincidence? I think not" vampire prince handed a scroll to a guard who stood beside him. The guard then passed it to the high king. The vampire prince told the high king that it was from the kingdom of old. It had been in his position since the end of the great war. Rebecca looked at him with a confused look and said, "the great war, but that would make you" before she could finish, the vampire prince replied, "yes, I am over 4000 years old" High King Laurence looked impressed. He opened the scroll and read it to himself. Immediately after reading the scroll, he decided without consulting the council that there was only one option. The scroll told of three spears that belonged to the three great gods, Zerthena, Zurothon, and Zaratheen. The king decided that gathering the spears was their only choice. These spears could be pieced together to form a trident, the very tool that originally banished Horrothors from the kingdom of old. The high king handed Rebecca the scroll, but it only told the location of the first spear. The scroll stated to get the spear, the one that sought it had to pass a trial to prove their worthiness. The first spear was in the dark forest, hidden from all but in plain sight. To acquire it, one must pass the test of a darkened heart. Rebecca asked what the test was, but even the vampire prince didn't know. Nevertheless, she agreed to take upon this quest and told her father with anxiousness. She would leave after she had rested and then raced out of the court. After Rebecca left, the vampire prince was about to leave when high king Laurence said, "before you leave may we ask, what is your name and why the sudden interest in helping", the vampire prince turned back to face the king smiled softly and said, "certainly, my name is Voinich the bloodthirsty and the reason for my help is simple, I like the arrangement I have with man it's peaceful, I like the peace" high king Laurence gave a single "ha" smiled and replied "well who would've thought it" the vampire prince then left with the intention to never convey with man again.

That evening the High King visited Alex. Alex was in his room in the high king's castle. He had his own room there because he liked to stay there more than he liked staying at his own home. While peacefully reading, he heard a knock on his door, Alex scuffled to straighten up his room before he answered the door, but King Laurence entered his room. Alex looked like he was up to something. In his boyish manner, he simply said, "yes!", King Laurence told Alex to sit with him, telling him they needed to speak. Alex was nervous. He was sure he was in trouble after his aunt and cousin saw him use magic. Alex was right, well... almost, King Laurence wanted to talk about his magic. While Alex sat on his bed next to King Laurence, the king told the young prince with a soft voice, "I know you have discovered that you have magic" speechless, Alex stammered, "er.. er.. er", "It's ok" said King Laurence, gently patting Alex on his back the high king stated "I think it's time you knew the truth" Alex looked shocked that wasn't what he expected, King Laurence told Alex that balomoor was right about his mother, but there was more to it, she was once kind and loving, but she began to practice dark magic. Over time she grew hateful and cared little for even herself. He told the young prince, "you see. All magic comes with a price, whether it be good magic or bad, some more than others pay the ultimate price" Alex looked to his grandfather. With tears in his eyes and a croke in his voice, he said, "like Aiden". Exactly said the high king "and like your mother", he added. Alex whacked King Laurence's hand away and raised his voice, saying, "you always told me she died in battle, so what is it" King Laurence walked over to Alex's window. He paused for a moment, then said "it happened just after you were born, your mother had been getting worse over the past year, and nothing we did would help; me, your grandmother, and your father pleaded with her to stop practising dark magic but, she had grown to a point where she no longer cared, I had no choice but to exile her according to the old laws, it was for you and your brother's safety. She did keep in contact with your father beyond the walls of my kingdom, and he even took you and your brother for days out in the castle gardens with her but, you were too young to remember the day she stopped coming, it was dark magic to grant immortality that took her in the end when you were around two cycles, we all thought it was for you and your brothers best interest, that we never told you the truth" Alex couldn't believe it, all the time they knew he had magic and kept it a secret, one thing passed his mind just one, Alex turned to his grandfather and at the top of his voice he screamed, bellowing through the corridor and down the hallways, "our best interest, our, best, interest, I'll tell you what was for our best interest, if we had a father who cared where we were, if you would of told us the truth about orcs, goblins and ogres rather than making us think they were myths, if you would of just told us the truth that we had magic, we could have been prepared that's what's in our best interest, if we had any of that Aiden would be safe" Alex then fell to his bed crying it was too much grief, King Laurence left the room he knew his grandson needed space. Alex waited until his grandparents were asleep, then went to his aunt's room, he needed someone to speak to, and they had built a bond over the days they spent together. He woke her and told her everything his grandfather told him. She already knew, of course, but Alex wasn't bothered. He had calmed down and just needed someone to comfort him. Rebecca and Alex decided that they would go on this quest together. At that moment in time, Alex wanted to be with someone he trusted, and being with his aunt was the best bet.

Chapter Six: Waking the beasts

The next day Alex and Rebecca prepared themselves at first light, as they were mounting their horses when King Laurence approached "Alex, what are you doing?" he asked "I'm going with Rebecca on this quest, I can't be here or with my father right now so, I'm going with my aunt and we will end this war before it begins," said Alex quite abruptly, while Alex made his final preparations King Laurence spoke to Rebecca "please watch out for him, I don't think he is taking things well", "of course," said Rebecca continuing to add "that is why he is coming with me", while Rebecca and the king were talking, Alex heard a familiar voice shout his name, he turned to see his younger cousin Noah running toward him, Noah worshipped Alex, in Noah's eyes Alex was already a king and could do no wrong, he was only two cycles younger than Alex but acted much younger, although at times Noah irritated Alex, Alex adored him he was his best friend and Alex knew Noah looked up to him, Noah threw his arms around Alex, hugged him and told Alex, he had heard all about his travels and that he had magic, Noah begged and pleaded for Alex to teach him magic but, Alex just told him he couldn't at that moment he had a very important matter to see to but, when he returned he would teach him all he knew. As the two began to ride, Alex felt horrible for lying to his cousin. He knew he wouldn't be able to teach him magic, but he couldn't break his heart. After all, he was so naive and had no clue how magic worked. Alex and Rebecca rode off, heading for the dark forest. As they approached the dark forest, Rebecca told Alex of the dangers that lay inside. She told him he could turn back if he wanted and told him no one would think any less of him and no one would make him go in. Alex didn't say a word. He just carried on. As they passed through the dark forest, it was empty. There was no walking dead, no wolfmen or spectres. There was nothing. Rebecca didn't like it. The forest was too empty, she told Alex she felt something was wrong, but he ignored her and pushed forward.

As they got deeper into the forest, they could hear growling and moaning. Alex carried on in the direction of the sounds. They came to a clearing, the walking dead surrounded the clearing, and the wolfmen were around the top. They were snarling and growling but not moving. Suddenly a spectre appeared. She was more beautiful than any woman in all the land, although she was pure white from head to toe, including her dress, "come closer, my children", said the spectre in a soft voice. Alex and Rebecca climbed off their horses and walked closer as if they were compelled by some unknown force, "what be your business in this dark place" said the spectre, "you're beautiful", said Alex moving closer, "what do you want riches, fame, glory I can give you it all, all you need do is ask" said the spectre in that soft voice, Alex asked the spectre for her name, "Lilith" replayed the spectre "Lilith, that's a beautiful name" said Alex becoming more entranced, Rebecca on the other hand; shook her head saying "this isn't right, something is wrong", "I know what you seek; your brother, I can return him if you wish" said Lilith "yes" said Alex jumping to the offer adding "I'll give anything", the spectre pointed to Alex's sword "that will be sufficient pay" she stated, Rebecca pulled out of her trance as Alex started to pull his sword from its sheff, she grabbed his sword lunged at Lilith and swung swiping through her smokey body, Lilith screamed and howled as she dissipated leaving the staff where she once stood, as Rebecca gripped the staff the wolf men ran of whimpering and the walking dead began to leave, Alex pulled out of his trance and asked Rebecca what happened, she told him as far as she can make out, the spectre Lilith prayed on his grief to try and trick him, Alex asked Rebecca how she knew it was a trick, she told him "her tricks affected you more that they affected me so I saw through them", Alex thanked Rebecca and they mounted their horses and made their way back to the kingdom of man. Back in the high king's castle, no one could work out what to do with the staff. Alex noticed something written on the staff, the high king summoned his graphologist who took the staff to analyse it, after several hours later the graphologist returned he had deciphered the writing, it read, to the east of desert land, lies the first house of man, there you will find what you seek, if your strength you can keep, Rebecca didn't want to waste any time she knew exactly where to go, King Laurence told her to wait until she and Alex had rested he told her they couldn't keep pushing themselves to their limits, the king was worried they were trying to fight this battle alone. After a good night's rest, Rebecca and Alex left for the dead deserts of despair. They didn't want anyone to stop them or make their quest last longer than it should, so they left before anybody else woke. When they arrived at the dead deserts of despair they stopped at the edge of the desert, Rebecca said to Alex "you should know that people are worried about you" Alex answered sharply "I know" Rebecca didn't want to push him but she had to get him to speak, "it wasn't your fault what happened to Aiden, you know that right" said Rebecca attempting to comfort him "I know" Alex snapped then pushed forward heading east of the desert, after several hours riding they came to a temple it looked older than anything they had ever seen, the stones look so old it seemed a single touch would bring the entire temple down, Rebecca told Alex to wait outside it was too dangerous for him, but he pushed past her and marched into the temple, Rebecca said to herself "something is wrong with him, it's more than just grief, it's something else", she caught up with Alex he was stood in the doorway of a large room the only thing in it was the staff, Alex walked over and grabbed the staff, as he did

Rebecca shouted "No, wait!" but it was too late, the room began to crumble around them; stood side by side they had no escape then Alex began to mutter something under his breath, Rebecca went to ask him what he said but before she could, Alex grabbed her wrist and screamed at the top of his lung the words "savrus persorem victorium vecks", a pulse of energy burst from Alex destroying the temple and blowing it in every direction, Alex dropped to his knees and begun to cry, suddenly it hit Rebecca she gripped Alex by his shoulders and told him "you have to stop using magic, the price your paying is emotional" Alex tried to pull away, saying no, but Rebecca wouldn't let him. She said, "Your magic is playing with your emotions, and you're losing control. Listen to me and stop using magic; I swear to you, we can win this without it" Alex nodded, wiping his tears away "okay", he said in a whimpering voice. They began making their way back to Broadhall, while they were travelling Rebecca did some much needed deep thought, she came to the conclusion she wasn't taking Alex with her to find the final staff, when they arrived at King Laurence's castle the grand high witch Susan was talking to King Laurence, Alex jumped of his horse and ran over to Susan, he flung his arms around her and began to cry, Susan shocked by the sudden burst of emotional affection said, "there, there child, what the heavens is the matter" but Alex just cried, Rebecca approach Susan and told her how they

57

couldn't save his brother, and his magic is playing with his emotions, "I see" said Susan sympathetically Alex took a step back; apologised and asked Susan what she was doing there, Susan told him the giants and trolls had become restless, she came to the king to seek refuge as she feared her home was no longer safe, Alex looked to his grandfather and simply said "well", is if implying he cannot refuse her refuge, King Laurence just nodded then walked away, Queen Clare took Susan to her room and Alex and Rebecca went with King Laurence. That evening the graphologist had deciphered the writing on the second staff but, Rebecca had spoken to King Laurence and told him, Alex wasn't to know what it said as she didn't want him going with her to get the final staff, she thought he needed to rest and get his emotions in check, King Laurence agreed, he told Alex to go to his room; Rebecca would let him know when they knew where to go and when she was ready to leave, Rebecca left the next morning before light even struck the land, Alex woke midday and rushed to get himself ready, King Laurence was waiting outside his room when he walked out, he told Alex he had something to show him, they when down into the dungeons Alex asked where they were going, King Laurence just told Alex to keep following him, they went deeper and deeper into the dungeons until, they came to a room with statues of all the previous kings around the room, King Laurence told Alex this was the tomb of once great kings, he told him one of the statues was of his father, he was taken from him not by battle, not by war but by a drunk man he was trying to help, Alex asked what this had to do with anything, King Laurence said Angrily "I'm getting to it", he told Alex that his father was a kind man that cared for everyone but himself then, he was struck down by one he tried to help, the king turned to Alex and said "you see boy, we have all lost someone we care about to evil, the evil in this world will always strife to snuff out the light but, our job is to hold that light in our hearts" he paused for a moment knelt down on one knee and said "do you understand", a single tear rolled down Alex's cheek, as he wiped it away he said "yes grandfather I understand", they both made their way back up to the castle, when they got back to the court yard Rebecca was returning with her soldiers staff in hand, Rebecca, Alex and the king took the third staff to the throne room where the other two staffs were, in the throne room each one of them took hold of a staff, the staffs began to pull as if they wanted to connect, they all let go of the staffs and in a blinding light, the three staffs crashed together forming the trident of the gods, Rebecca went to pick the trident of the floor but it burnt her hand, King Laurence placed a rag over the trident and picked it up stating "I figured as much, only those truly worthy can wield the Trident", Rebecca holding her burnt hand said with a sarcastic yet angry tone "well that would have been good to know", she carried on to say "how exactly am I meant to prove my worthiness", the king just shrugged and said with a chuckle "hell if I know", at that moment Susan walked in and told them she might be able to help, she told them of a cave high on the peak of the caved mountains, it was the home of the four elemental dragons, Rebecca said angrily "we can't go there, that is the home of the vamp..er..haemonemics, if we step foot on those mountains we break the truce with the haemonemics, that truce has stood for centuries", Susan told her that she would send word to the vampire prince, informing him why they would be there, Rebecca didn't like it but there didn't seem to be any other option, Rebecca asked how they were meant to get to the peak of the caved mountains, Alex jumped in saying "I have a way, I know someone who can help" Rebecca hesitantly agreed, they prepared themselves for another quest, one Rebecca feared could go horribly wrong, while they mounted their horses in the courtyard Jayden ran over to Alex, "let me come with you I can help" pleaded Jayden, Alex gave Jayden his sword and said "your needed here, if I don't return you're going to have to protect our family", Jayden took the sword and just nodded with that and Alex and Rebecca rode of. Alex led Rebecca to the kingdom of beasts, "what are we doing here?" she asked, just as she asked Thermasol landed beside them, Rebecca drew here sword and told Alex to move away from the beast, Thermasol asked Rebecca who she was calling a beast, shocked Rebecca said "it can talk", Alex told Rebecca to lower her sword and told her he was his friend, Alex told Thermasol they needed his help, he told Alex he already knew the light spirits had already told him, Thermasol bowed his head and said "please accept my condolences on your brother's fate, it was a grave sorrow to hear what happened" Alex hugged Thermasol and told him not to worry, he asked him if he would take them to the peak for the caved mountains, Thermasol nodded and told them to climb on his back, he took flight to the caved mountains, while they traveled Thermasol said "the light spirits told me, the young prince has learnt some new skills", Alex told Thermasol about his magic, he told him about his travels and the things he's seen, Thermasol said "a lot has happened my young prince since we last met, but know this, no matter what happens next retain your good heart, that is and will always be your strongest weapon, it will be a valuable asset against the forces of evil" Alex took in what Thermasol said, he knew his friend only ever meant good, he wouldn't tell him something he didn't think would help. When they arrived at the peak of the caved mountains, Thermasol landed outside a cave, and Alex and Rebecca went in. The only thing in the cave was a large stone circle, the circle, although in one piece, was split into four segments one red, one white, one green, and one blue. In the centre of each segment was a smaller stone circle with a dragon carved into

61

them, in the centre of the whole thing was an empty glass vial, along the top was writing in a strange language, Rebecca told Alex she knew the language but, it had been sometime since she would have known what it said, Alex asked her how long it would take for her to remember how to read it, she told him to give her sometime, Alex was getting frustrated he shouted at her saying "we don't have time for this", Rebecca shouted back at him telling him to sit down and shut up, a few minutes later Rebecca told Alex she knew what it said she told him it read, "only the tear of the beast can't wake the beast" Alex said "that's easy" he grabbed the vial and ran outside to Thermasol, he ask him if he could give him some tears to wake the dragons, Thermasol forced a few tears out for Alex to catch in the vial, Alex ran back in and put the vial back in the centre but nothing happened, he asked Rebecca why it wasn't working, she told him she didn't know but she would figure it out, Alex went back to Thermasol and told him to take him back to Broadhall, they took flight leaving Rebecca in the cave, as they landed back in Broadhall the king's guards watched as they came down from the sky, to them it looked as if Alex was just flying through the air, one of the guards said to Alex "what sort of magic is this", just then King Laurence walked out of the castle doors "marvellous a real live griffin, I have never seen one before, this is fantastic" he chuckled with excitement, "where is Susan" Alex said taking no time to pause, "In her room but" Alex ran off before his grandfather could finish speaking leaving him astounded with Thermasol, Alex burst in to Susan's room ranting about a tear, Susan told him to calm down and asked what the problem was, after Alex explained, Susan reached in her bag and passed him a small vial with a single drop of liquid init, she told him it was a dragon's tear, she hoped to keep it for a potion but it's seemed to have found its own use, Alex thanked her and ran back to Thermasol, as they took flight the king asked what he was doing but, he just replied "I don't have time" and took off back to the caved mountains, when they landed Rebecca demanded to know what he was doing, she told him she turned around and he was gone, Alex explained that he went to see Susan and she gave him a dragon tear, he went to put the vial in the centre of the stone circle but, black smoke began to fill the floor, they heard a voice it was familiar but it had a manic growl to it, "you pathetic, diotic fools" the voice said, the smoke began to build a pillar in front of them, then in a flash of black light stood before them was none other than Aiden, "are you still running around like a pair of Imbeciles" said Aiden with that manic growling tone, the darkness had completely taken over him, Alex stepped forward and told Aiden he was going to find a way to reverse what happened to him, Aiden said aggressively in that same manic tone "take another step and I'll rip you limb from limb", Alex shocked by the way his brother was acting said "Aiden this isn't you", Aiden looked at Alex grinned and said "it is now why, don't you like the new me", before Alex could answer Aiden said "it doesn't matter this is me now and, as for reversing it, you even try and I'll turn you inside out", it was clear to Alex and Rebecca the darkness had driven Aiden insane, Rebecca asked Aiden why he was acting the way he was and, what was wrong with his voice, Aiden said with a grin "say hello to your new resident chaos demon", Alex accepted in that moment his brother was lost to the darkness that consumed him, Rebecca asked Aiden if he was there to stop them, Aiden told her there was no point; they were never going to stop the God of death so it was pointless, he just wanted to have some fun scaring them, with that Aiden clicked his fingers and vanished in a flash of black light, Rebecca told Alex there was nothing they could do for Aiden, they should carry on trying to awaken the dragons, Alex just nodded and put the vial in the stone circle, as soon as he did the ground began to shake, white smoke burst from the stone circle, the smoke then turned to fire, then water ran from the circle and along the floor out of the cave, Alex and Rebecca followed the water out of the cave, it ran straight off the cliff into the air like a floating stream, the four elements began to circle around each other in the air; fire, water, earth and air spinning faster and faster until, they exploded momentarily blinding Alex, Rebecca and Thermasol, as they regained their sight before them were the four elemental dragons, the dragons spoke to Alex and Rebecca telepathically, as they spoke one would start the sentence and another would finish it, they asked Rebecca and Alex why they were summoned, Rebecca told them they needed their help, she explained that Horrothors had risen in the valley of the damned and he was building an army, she told them that they had constructed the trident of the gods but, no one could hold it. Rebecca asked the dragons if they could tell here how to become worthy, the dragons told Rebecca she would never be worthy but another would, they said "when the final blow is struck, the one who is worthy will know, only then can they hold the trident and banish Horrothors", with that the dragons flew into the skies above, both Rebecca and Alex had no clue what to do next, the dragons left them with more questions than answers, nevertheless they went home there was nothing more for them there, they climbed on Thermasol and took flight, when they arrived back in Broadhall; in the throne room they told King Laurence, Queen Clare and Susan what the dragons told them, Susan began to pace back and forth the king asked her why she was so bothered, Susan said with a slight tremble in her voice, "it's as I feared, the final battle is upon us, Alex and Rebecca must face Horrothors", Queen Clare stood from her throne; raising her voice she said "my grandson is not facing a god in battle he's fourteen, he's still a child" King Laurence tried to calm her but it wasn't working, she told the king if he aloud his grandson to go to battle she was leaving him, King Laurence was stuck between allowing his kingdom to fall or allowing his marriage to fail, Alex stood and told his grandfather and his grandmother he was going to fight, Queen Clare walked out of the throne room, Alex told his grandfather he was going to prepare himself, he left the throne room and the king followed after the queen.

Chapter Seven: The final battle

The following morning Alex and Rebecca prepared themselves to face Horrothors. They were in the courtyard with Thermasol, loading everything they needed on Thermasol. Jayden approached Alex and passed him his sword. He told him he was going to need it to fight the Orcs, Alex thanked him, and Jayden hugged him, he told him he was the bravest person he ever knew, and he was proud to be his cousin. Just then, Queen Clare walked out of the castle carrying a large bag and climbed into a carriage. Alex asked where she was going. She told Alex she loved him, but she couldn't be around his grandfather. With that, she left. Jayden told him she was going to Queen Bethany's palace. Rebecca told Alex they had to leave they climbed on Thermasol's back and took flight, while they were on their way to the valley of the damned, Thermasol asked if they had a plan, Rebecca said "we're going to destroy this beast any way we can", Alex was nervous he hadn't felt the way he did since it all began, he told Thermasol he wasn't sure how they were going to defeat Horrothors but, they weren't going to stop until they did, Thermasol landed just of the valley of the damned as Alex and Rebecca climbed off Thermasol he said to the young prince "I think this may be our final farewell my friend, if so know this, not all weapons are designed to kill, if you use your heart and mind all battle can be won, now farewell young prince and good luck", with that Thermasol took flight disappearing into the clouds, Alex and Rebecca began making their way into the valley, they used the same route they used when they rescued Jayden, but it was dead there was no goblins or ogres and not an orc in sight, they moved slowly through the valley the red glow in the distance got brighter as they got further in, they could see the opening to the clearing at the end of the valley but still they hadn't seen any sign of life, as they walked into the clearing there was Horrothors stood larger than life, he laughed as the two walked into the clearing, "you've come to slay me have you" said Horrothors as he laughed, "it's a shame your all that's left" he said, Alex asked what he meant by all that's left, Horrothors laughed then said "my army have gone to wipe your land clean, soon you two will be all that remain", Rebecca screamed "I'm going to send you back to wherever it is you came from, you're a parasite, a waste of life, I don't know how anything would have allowed you to live when you were born", Horrothors scowled then through a ball of fire at Rebecca and Alex, Rebecca lifted the enchanted shield which created a barrier stopping Horrothors's attack, Horrothors then began throwing ball after ball of fire but it couldn't break the barrier, suddenly a wormling swooped down and pulled the shield from Rebecca's hand, Rebecca took a long item of her back wrapped in cloth, she began to unwrap it, it was the trident, "no it can't be" said Horrothors moving backwards, "how can you have that, it is supposed to be in the kingdom of old" he said with a hint of fear, Rebecca gripped the trident and it began to burn her, she held on for as long as she could while trying to hide her pain, but she couldn't hold on, she dropped the trident and gripped her burnt hand, her fingers had fused together and the skin on her hand had all but burnt down to the bone, Horrothors laughed realising she couldn't wield the trident, he raised his hand as if about to crush Rebecca, Alex stood in front of Rebecca and said "I hate you, I hate your army, I hate everything you have done, you have ruined everything", the wind began to blow but all sound seemed to leave the land all apart from Alex's voice, as he screamed at the top of his voice while anger filled his heart "savrus persorem victorium vecks", pulse after pulse of energy shot from Alex's hands shooting directly for horrothors, but the God just laughed, he then rose fire from the ground and Rebecca through Alex out of the way, the flames engulfed Rebecca in a hellish inferno when the flames died down all that remained was the trident, Alex was mortified Horrothors had destroyed his aunt, but Alex didn't cry or become scared, instead he stood up walked over to the glowing red trident then picked it up, the trident instantly cooled as he gripped it, "I am worthy" he said with absolutely no emotion, he took a crystal out of his pocket, the same one Susan had given him when he left the forest of Eeldoor, Horrothors began raising fire from the ground but, the trident was protecting Alex and he wasn't scared, Horrothors began ripping Arcadia apart, creating earthquakes that ripped the land apart. Alex through the trident at Horrothors, hitting him straight in the chest. He then gripped the crystal tightly, saying, "take me somewhere safe" Alex vanished in a flash of bright light, Horrothors collapsed to the ground, and his flesh began to crumble and blow away like hot ash. The God had been defeated, and with one final attempt, he caused an earthquake so powerful it cracked Arcadia. The earthquake shattered the land into smaller masses of land. As the land shattered, Horrothors's army had just reached the dwarf kingdom. The land opened up in front of the army, stopping them from being able to attack the dwarf kingdom. In the kingdom of man, High King Laurence, King David, and King Adam, with their soldiers, tried to protect the people from the collapsing buildings. The rest of the royal families huddled for safety in the high king vault. The land shattered crevices opened up and filled with the seas. The landmasses moved further apart. The kingdoms were separated Arcadia was no more. Alex appeared on a beach the waves were crashing, the wind was gently blowing and birds squawked overhead it was peaceful, Alex stood looking over the sea, suddenly Aiden appeared to his side "greetings brother" he said, Alex thought something was different, it was his voice, it no longer had that manic growl to it, "do you know what happened" Aiden asked, "yes I was fighting Horrothors he was winning, I couldn't win so, I stabbed him with the trident and used the crystal" said Alex slightly disoriented, he paused for a moment then asked "why are we here" Aiden sighed deep then said, "that was fifteen thousand cycles back or as people today call it, fifteen thousand years", Alex looked to Aiden and said "are you still" but before he could end his sentence Aiden replied "no, it took five thousand years but I'm not evil, I protect man now" Alex looked at his brother then looked back out at sea, "why are you still a boy" he asked, Aiden explained his curse makes him immortal but also stops him from aging, Alex asked him why he felt so strange, Aiden told him it was probably because of the jump in time, Aiden asked what actually happened in that final moment, Alex told him he asked the crystal to take him somewhere safe, "ah that must be it, with everything that was happening, the crystal brought you to the first time evil hasn't threatened the world" said Aiden, Alex paused; thought for a moment then asked what happened to their family, Aiden went quiet he took a deep breath then said "unfortunately they all perished, they thought they would be safe in the high kings vault but, it collapsed and killed them all, well apart from Laurence, David and Adam, they stayed behind to protect the people, Laurence fell in battle; David and Adam were crushed by falling buildings," Alex didn't know what to say, he remained silent for a moment then said "it was all for nothing then" Aiden put his hand on Alex's shoulder and said cheerfully as if to cheer his brother up, "no, no, no it wasn't all for nothing, more than half of the people survived all thanks to their brave leaders, and the forces of evil were destroyed when the dark god horrothors was destroyed" Alex smiled, he could tell his brother was trying to make him feel better, the two sat there for what seemed like forever then Alex asked Aiden what they do next, Aiden simply told him with a smile and his hand on Alex's shoulder they live. The two brothers sat there looking out to sea until the sun began to set. By morning they were gone. It's not known what happened to the brothers, but it would be nice to think they lived a good life. Maybe Alex met a woman and had a family, and the two brothers lived a good life until Alex passed from old age. Maybe Aiden wonders the world doing good. We never know, but one thing can be said, the land that time long forgot will always live on in those that want to remember.